WHAT
DO
REAL
PiGEONS
EAT?

Farshore

REAL PIGEONS
EAT DANGER!

TUMBLER
so bendy!

HOMEY
directions
champ!

CONTENTS

'Mmm . . . pie!'

CHAPTER 1

At the centre of the city, in a wide open square,

there is something
very awesome.

It's just a statue.

But if you look closely,
you can see something
even more awesome
than a lion . . .

A PIGEON!

His name is Rock.

He belongs to
a squad of
crime-fighting
heroes called

**REAL
PiGEONS.**

The squad is having the day off, because even heroes need to relax sometimes.

Grandpouter is **reading**.

Homey is **resting**.

And Frillback and Tumbler are doing some **FEATHER BOXING**. It's like fighting but with tickles instead of punches.

'The winner will be the **FEATHERWEIGHT CHAMPION**.'

But Rock loves fighting crime so much that he's keeping watch, just in case there is trouble.

REAL PIGEONS
HEADQUARTERS

stinky alley

UNDERGROUND CARPARK

yum! donuts!

And trouble soon comes.

A fox bounds across the town square.

He is chewing a twig. Or at least, he's trying to.

'Uh-oh!' says the fox.

The twig is stuck.

But if Rock flies down to help, the fox will rip him apart.

After all, Rock *is* a bird. And foxes eat birds.

Luckily, Rock is also a
MASTER OF DISGUISE.

So he flies to a tree and rubs sap
on his wings and legs.

He borrows a red
scarf from an
old lady.

'I'll bring this back
in a moment!'

And finds a bin with
broken eggshells inside.

'Eggshells
make great
teeth!'

9

Now Rock is a fox too.

He walks across the town square . . .

PLUCK!

. . . and removes the twig.

'Thanks. I'm Red Fox and snacks aren't usually that much trouble,'

says Red Fox.

'Leave wood-eating to beavers and termites!'

Rock has saved the fox **AND** the twig.

Red Fox takes off.

'Anyway, bye!'

Rock looks closely at the twig.
Pigeons adore twigs.

Twigs make pigeons feel warm and good. Like when you drink a hot chocolate or snuggle into your grandma's dressing gown.

'I will call you **TRENT**,' Rock says to the twig.

Rock and Trent have terrific fun together.

They play dress-ups.

'Moustaches don't tickle at all!'

They share a meal.

'I'll eat whatever you don't eat, Trent!'

And they chase a fly, just for fun.

'Come back here, you flying booger!'

Until the other **REAL PIGEONS** swoop down from the sky.

'Greetings, PIGS!' cries Homey.

'We're going to the laundry,' says Grandpouter. 'To ride in the tumble dryers and fluff up our feathers. Want to come?'

But Rock hardly notices. He has a **funny feeling** Trent could be a **SECRET WEAPON.**

'Hey squad,' says Rock. 'What do you think of twigs?'

'**Twigs are COO!**'

says Frillback.

'I ate a twig once,' says Homey.

'I mistook it for a very small breadstick.'

'Mmmmm.'

'Twigs are the fingernails of trees,' says Tumbler.

'Hmmm.'

'Come on, squad,' says Frillback. 'My feathers need a blow-tumble-dry.'

The others fly off. Rock shakes his head. He's being silly. A twig can't be a **SECRET WEAPON**.

'I'd better set you free, Trent,' says Rock sadly. 'You'll be happier on the ground covered in dead leaves anyway.'

Rock takes Trent back to where they first met.

Where he makes a shocking discovery.

'That bird is **STUCK IN A BOTTLE!**' cries Rock.

CHAPTER 2

There are lots of things that belong in bottles.

soft drink

genies

'WISHES!!!'

ships

But **NOT** birds.

This poor bird can't move. He can't even open his beak enough to talk. He looks mad.

'Why are you in a bottle?' asks Rock. 'I'm going to get help!'

He flies as fast as he can to the laundry.

Where he finds the pigeons inside tumble dryers, fluffing their feathers.

'**This is weird,**' says Tumbler.

'Squad, you'll never believe what I've found!' says Rock.

Tumbler sees Trent. 'Still got that twig, huh?' she says.

Rock was so worried about the bottled bird that he totally forgot to free Trent. Maybe it's a sign?

'Actually,' says Rock, 'my **pigeon instinct** is telling me this twig could be a SECRET WEAPON!'

'How can a twig be a **SECRET WEAPON?**'

'My muscles are the only **SECRET WEAPON** I care about.'

'I don't know,' says Rock, 'but right now we have a **BIRD-MERGENCY.** Follow me. HURRY!'

Rock rushes the pigeons back to the bird in the bottle.

'I know this bird!' says Grandpouter. 'He's a spoonbill. His name is **Bill Spoon**. He lives by the pond and wouldn't have climbed into a bottle. Someone must have **forced** him in.'

'What kind of monster bottles a bird?' says Frillback.

'We need to get Bill out of there!' adds Rock. 'And hunt down the bird-bottler!'

'REAL PIGEONS STOP BIRD-BOTTLERS!'

The squad tries to help Bill Spoon.

'I'm going to smash the glass,' says Frillback. **'Let's free Bill now!'**

'NO!' cries Tumbler.

'You might cut Bill. Or yourself. It's too dangerous.'

SCAN
SCAN
SCAN
SCAN
SCAN
SCAN

Rock and Trent scan the bottle for clues.

'Spoonbills eat fish,' says Grandpouter.

'But he looks like he hasn't eaten for ages. Homey, could you please fetch a fish?'

'Coo coo!' says Homey.

SCAN
SCAN
SCAN
SCAN
SCAN
SCAN
SCAN

Homey flies off.

'That fish is too eaten.'

'That one's too alive.'

CHOMP!

CHOMP!

CHOMP!

FISH FINGERS

'These ones are covered in breadcrumbs. **PERFECT!**'

He brings one back to hungry Bill.

Meanwhile, Rock has found a clue.
'This is a recycled bottle,' he says.

'I've seen big recycling trucks going down the lane behind the town square,' says Frillback.

'Maybe that's where this bottle came from?'

'Go investigate,' says Grandpouter.

'Tumbler and I will keep Bill Spoon company.'

Homey, Frillback and Rock (and Trent) go down the lane and arrive at a skip.

It smells terrible.

Like rotten porridge made with old milkshakes.

'Hey!' cries Rock.

'This slice of bread looks just like Homey!'

'PIG this! Dude that!'

'Give me myself – I'm hungry!'

'Hello there, birdos!'

An ibis appears.
'I'm Straw Neck,' she says.
'What are you doing
at my skip?'

'A bird is stuck in a bottle,' says Rock.
'We're hunting down the bird-bottler!'

'You must be the new hero-birdos,'
says Straw Neck. 'I've heard about you.'

'That's us – we're the **REAL PIGEONS!**'
says Rock proudly.

But Straw Neck doesn't
look impressed.

'Well, I'm an **INVENTOR**,' says Straw Neck. She hops down and shows off some of her inventions.

A PORTABLE BIRD BATH

sink

suitcase on wheels

pogo stick

VACUUM CLEANER SCOOTER

scooter

vacuum cleaner

toaster

'I give my inventions to birds who need them,' explains Straw Neck. 'Like Marcel. He sprained his ankle when he bent down to get the first worm one morning.'

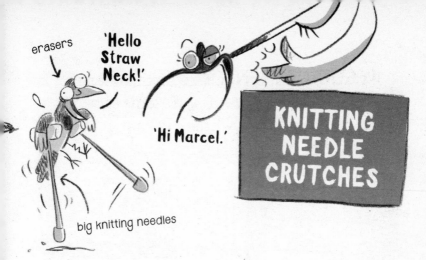

erasers

'Hello Straw Neck!'

'Hi Marcel.'

KNITTING NEEDLE CRUTCHES

big knitting needles

'That's amazing,' cries Homey. 'You find all the bits and pieces for these inventions in the dumpster?'

Straw Neck shrugs. 'Mostly.'

'My knitting!'

'My pogo!'

'My wheels!'

'Sometimes you have to be **BAD** to be **GOOD**,' adds Straw Neck.

Rock isn't sure about that.

It's **GOOD** that Straw Neck's inventions help birds like Marcel. But it's **BAD** that she borrows things without asking.

'Hey, Straw Neck,' says Rock. 'Isn't it called **STEALING** when you take something without –'

'Oh my gosling! Is that your PET STICK?' interrupts Straw Neck, pointing at Trent.

Rock goes red.

'I think Trent might be a **SECRET WEAPON**,' he protests. 'But right now we're trying to find whoever stuffed Bill Spoon into a bottle.'

'Straw Neck, where do humans take bottles for recycling?' asks Frillback.

'Look behind the skip,' says Straw Neck.

The pigeons follow her directions.

And find . . .

... three more bottled birds.

Rock can see they have been greased in butter. And jammed into bottles.

heron

duck

goldfinch

'Someone is bottling **LOTS** of birds,' says Rock in dismay.

'It's true,' says an echoey voice.

It's the goldfinch.

His beak is small and isn't stuck shut, so he can speak from inside the bottle.

'I didn't see who did it,' says the goldfinch, 'because they bopped me on the head.'

Rock can't believe it.

'Don't worry, birds,' he says. 'We'll get you out. And stop whoever is doing this!'

'Let's take these birds back to the others,' says Frillback.

Using her super strength, she gathers up the bottles and they all take off.

'Mmm, me bread.'

But when they get back to the town square, they discover three bad things.

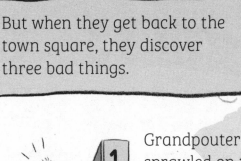

1. Grandpouter is sprawled on the ground.

2. The bottle with Bill Spoon inside is missing.

3. AND TUMBLER IS GONE.

'WHERE IS BENDY, FRIENDLY TUMBLER?'

cries Frillback.

CHAPTER 3

Frillback helps Grandpouter sit up.

He is muttering weird things.

'I saw socks running away.
The big cat ate the bird.
Merry Christmas everyone!'

'Someone must have bopped him on the head too,' says Frillback. 'And taken off with Bill and Tumbler!'

Rock is frightened. He hugs Trent close.

But Rock can't hug Trent *and* help Grandpouter. Even if Trent is special somehow.

So Rock makes a hard decision.

'**Sorry, Trent,**'
he says.

'I don't know if you are a **SECRET WEAPON** or not. But I have to help my pigeon pals now.'

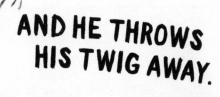

AND HE THROWS HIS TWIG AWAY.

poor Trent!

'Are you OK, Grandpouter?' says Rock.

Grandpouter nods slowly.

'The big cat ate the bird!'
he says again.

RUMBLE

'Why does he keep saying that?' asks Frillback.

'I don't know,' says Rock, worried. 'And we still have no idea who the bird-bottler is. Or where Tumbler and Bill Spoon are.'

This case is going from **bad** to **worse**.

'I'm still hungry, PIGS,' says Homey. 'Since there are no breadcrumbs here, maybe I'll try eating a twig again.'

Twigs are not tasty. And they can cause fights.

'TWO CAN PLAY WITH WOOD!'

'I didn't mean to hit you ...'

As Frillback and Homey fight, Grandpouter rubs his head.

'The big cat ate the bird!'

he says, a third time.

'Oh,' cries Rock, jumping up. 'I know what he's trying to say.'

He zooms up into the air, leaving the others behind.

'Grandpouter saw where **Bill Spoon** went,' says Rock.

'He's saying that someone put the bottle in the lion's mouth!'

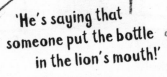

Rock lands on the lion's stone tongue.

The bottle isn't there.

The back of the lion's throat is very dark.

'Maybe someone hid Bill Spoon back here?'

Rock takes two steps forward and suddenly the ground disappears.

ROCK FALLS DOWN, DOWN, DOWN...

... and lands on a big, soft mattress.

He has fallen through the lion statue's body, and all the way down a secret tunnel to an underground warehouse.

There are **HUNDREDS** of bottled birds. Seagulls, magpies, robins, wrens, ducks, egrets – and many more.

Rock can't believe it.

'The bird-bottler is out of control!'

Then Rock spots Bill Spoon . . . and Tumbler! His heart jumps inside his feathery chest.

Suddenly, a familiar voice echoes through the warehouse.

'PIGEON! WHERE DID YOU COME FROM?'

IT'S RED FOX.

The fox that tried to eat Trent.

'So you found the tunnel I dug!' cries Red Fox.

'THAT'S BAD LUCK!'

Red Fox must be the bird-bottler.

Rock wishes he had a disguise. Or Trent, to shove back in the fox's mouth.

'Are you going to eat me?' asks Rock, trembling.

'No, I think it's time you went in a bottle,' sneers the fox, inching closer.

'Besides, I'm vegetarian.'

Rock stalls for time. 'If you don't eat animals, why are you doing this?' he asks.

'I just do what the **MANAGER** tells me,' snarls the fox. 'Which is to butter up birds and shove them in bottles. Except for Tumbler, who went in with no butter at all!'

'Who is the **MANAGER?**' asks Rock.

Red Fox doesn't answer.

He pounces.

PLUCK!

Rock quickly shoves some of his feathers into Red Fox's mouth.

'Noooooo, I'm vegetarian!' yells the fox.

As Red Fox chokes on the feathers, Rock sees a big jar full of coins.

BUY A BIRD WITH A GOLD COIN

← human money

Now Rock understands **EVERYTHING**.
'This warehouse is a **BIRD SHOP!**' he cries.

'That's right,' splutters Red Fox.

'The **MANAGER** pays me in seeds and nuts. They're much safer to eat than twigs.'

The whole **BIRD SHOP** operation is now clear.

birds bottled here

bottled birds slide down lion's throat

tunnel dug by fox

bottled birds waiting to be sold

bottled birds land here

48

Meanwhile, up in the town square,
Frillback and Homey have stopped fighting.
And started a game of baseball.

Grandpouter is finally feeling better. 'Pigeons!'
he says. 'Don't you see what's happening
here?'

'We're playing a game instead of fighting
crime?' asks Frillback.

'No!' says Grandpouter. 'Your twigs have turned out to be **SECRET WEAPONS**. And I've remembered where Tumbler and Bill were taken!'

'The big cat! Its mouth must lead somewhere. **COME ON!**'

They're about to fly up when another bird appears.

'Good, I found you birdos!'

It's Straw Neck, the ibis.

What does she want?

Down in the **BIRD SHOP**, Rock is disgusted. What kind of creature sells bottled birds? And what kind of human would buy them?

The kind that's just walked in through the front door, that's who!

'I'm here to buy some birds.'

'YOU HAVE **NO RIGHT** TO BUY BIRDS! WHY DON'T YOU GO AWAY. **SHOO!**'

'This angry little pigeon is adorable. I was looking for blackbirds. But maybe I'll take this guy instead.'

The woman reaches for Rock. But then,
a scream pierces the air.

'Oh-

-My-

-Gosling!'

Straw Neck has arrived.

'Are **YOU** the **MANAGER?**' cries Rock.

'Um . . . no,' says Straw Neck. 'It's not just pigeons who can be heroes, you know!'

She holds up a weird tool.

hairdryer

sharp bits

battery

'I invented a glass cutter,' she says.

'I thought you could use it to free the bottled birds.'

'That's **GOOD,** but squashing me is **BAD!**' wheezes Rock.

Suddenly, more birds come flying out of the tunnel.

IT'S THE **REAL PIGEONS!**

55

Frillback flaps up to Rock. 'Your **PIGEON INSTINCT** was right,' she says. 'Twigs can be a **SECRET WEAPON.**'

'And we brought yours with us!' says Homey, pulling a twig out of his feathers.

'Trent!'

Rock wraps his friend in a big, feathery hug. Rock still doesn't know exactly how Trent is a **SECRET WEAPON**. He's just happy to have his twig back again.

But behind them, DANGER LURKS.

'More funny little pigeons,'
says the woman, striding over.
'I'll buy all of them!'

'I don't think so,' cries Frillback,
swinging her log
at the woman.

PEW!

PEW!
PEW!

Homey follows up
with a twig-ball attack.

57

'ENOUGH OF THIS!'
cries Red Fox, pouncing
at the pigeons.

But with a quick jab, Frillback
pins the fox to the wall.

'Your bad bird
shop is finished,'
she says.

'Actually,' says Rock, 'the shop
belongs to the **MANAGER**.
And I've just figured
out who it is!'

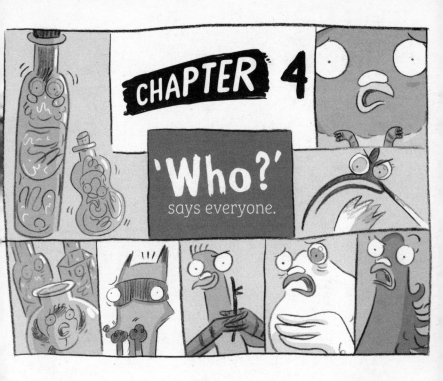

'Red Fox said he squeezed Tumbler into a bottle without butter,' explains Rock, 'because she is very flexible. And I remembered there was **one other** bird in a bottle who wasn't **buttery**. A bird who can pay Red Fox in seeds and nuts. A bird who is the **MANAGER**. That bird is ...'

NO BUTTER

'... THE GOLDFINCH!'

Everyone gasps.

'Yes, it was me!' admits the goldfinch.
'I've been catching, bottling and selling birds.
I hid in an empty bottle when you pigeons
caught me behind the skip.'

'You could fly
out of there this
whole time?'

'I can't believe
we were carrying
around a criminal!'

'I could have
solved this mystery
if I wanted to.'

There's just one thing Rock doesn't understand.

'Why do you want money?' he says. 'Animals don't need to buy things.'

'I don't **spend** the money,' says the goldfinch. 'I just **collect** it. Gold is my favourite colour. My friends call me Gold*pinch*!'

'Birds are weird.'

'MWAHAHAHAHA!'

Goldpinch gives Rock a nasty look.

'Now I will sell all of you too!'

'You can't sell us!' laughs Frillback. 'You're completely outnumbered!'

But Goldpinch grabs three bird eggs from a shelf.

'I've decided to start stealing bird eggs and putting them in bottles,' he says with a cackle.

'I'll never have to butter another bird, because they'll be trapped the moment they hatch!'

PURE EVIL!

Then he points to a large jar on the shelf.

'Now get inside,' he threatens.

'Or I'll smash these eggs. This is NO YOLK!'

FOR BIG BIRDS

Rock starts to sweat.

He can't allow Goldpinch to smash the eggs. Or put them in a bottle to hatch.

It's time to use Trent.

'Hold it right there, you small, devilish bird!'

Goldpinch laughs. 'I'm not afraid of your twig, Rock. It's not a **SECRET WEAPON**. No matter what you say.'

But Rock has always had a **FUNNY FEELING** about Trent. And his squad thinks he's right. So maybe he is.

He waves Trent in the air.

'The joke's on you, Goldpinch,' says Rock.
'My twig is a **SECRET WEAPON** after all.'

'What kind of weapon is it?'

Rock grins.
'A WEAPON OF MASS **DISTRACTION!**'

Goldpinch spins around. '**NOOOOO!**'

While Rock has been distracting Goldpinch, Straw Neck is cutting holes in bottles – with her glass cutter!

THE BIRDS ARE . . . .

FINALLY FREE!

And the eggs are saved!

'Thank you,' says Bill Spoon, shaking Rock's wing. 'Your squad has saved the day!'

But Straw Neck is not so happy.

'They didn't save the day – **I DID!**' she says, grumpily.

Goldpinch and Red Fox try to sneak off, but Bill Spoon seizes them.

SNAP!

SNAP!

'What are we going to do with these two villains?' says Rock.

'I will teach them how to be good at the pond,' says Bill.

'And I'll return those unhatched eggs on the way.'

'**WAIT!** My gold coins!'

'Let it go, Goldpinch. I've always wanted to go to school!'

'Come on,' says Grandpouter. 'We don't want to miss it.'

'Miss what?' says Rock.

'The view!' cries Grandpouter. 'There is nothing more beautiful than watching birds go free!'

And there really isn't.

THE END . . . FOR NOW

BUT SOMETIMES,

BIRDS GOING FREE IS NOT SO BEAUTIFUL.

Sometimes, it's bad.

Because just a few blocks away . . .

THERE IS A CRIMINAL OSTRICH.

CHAPTER 1

One of life's simple pleasures is finding a good piece of **STRING**.

Especially if you're a pigeon.

It doesn't even have to be string. It can just be a **STRINGY THING**.

Like a shoelace

or a piece of wool,

or the last hair that falls from a balding man's head.

'I'm stressed!'

Usually, pigeons use **STRINGY THINGS** to make nests.

But today Rock is weaving **STRINGY THINGS** together for a different reason.

He is making special gifts for the **REAL PIGEONS**.

'Thanks for the help, Trent,' says Rock.

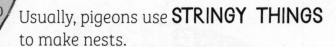

He finds the squad on the gazebo roof.

'I made **FRIENDSHIP BANDS!**' cries Rock. 'You guys aren't just crime-fighters. You're also my best friends.'

The pigeons are overjoyed.

'**I ALWAYS** wanted a friendship band made from **STRINGY THINGS!**' cries Tumbler.

'Put them around your ankles,' says Rock, 'because we don't have wrists!'

Rock ties one of the bands around Grandpouter's ankle.

'And it's all thanks to you, Grandpouter!' says Rock. 'You got the **REAL PIGEONS** squad together in the first place!'

REAL PIGEONS are REAL FRIENDS

'Neat!' says Grandpouter. 'I haven't changed my look since I fell into a bucket of blue paint ten years ago.'

The pigeons all fly down to the ground.

'Now, let's start our **SQUAD MEETING**,' says Grandpouter.

Today he is teaching them some **CRIME-FIGHTING** tricks.

'I have been fighting crime for a long time,' he tells them. 'There are three things you should always do.'

'And **#3:** crime-fighters should **EAT DANGER**,' finishes Grandpouter.

'Wait, what?' says Frillback.

Grandpouter smiles. 'You don't always need super strength or twigs to fight crime. Sometimes all you need is **your beak**.'

'I can't wait to **EAT DANGER**. Maybe I'll find a loaf of bread shaped like an axe. Or a baguette that looks like a snake!'

But before the pigeons can **EAT DANGER**, they are interrupted by two small voices.

'Excuse us!' says a field mouse.

'We need your help!' cries a lizard.

'What's wrong?' asks Rock.

'**A CRIMINAL OSTRICH** has broken out of the ostrich farm,' says the mouse.

'Ostriches love to eat little guys like us,' adds the lizard. 'We came to you because we heard **REAL PIGEONS** fight crime.'

'Do you have any more information about the ostrich?' asks Grandpouter.

'We have a phone that someone lost in the park.' The mouse shows them. 'The ostrich has made the news.'

BEWARE!
CRIMINAL OSTRICH ON THE LOOSE.

A dangerous ostrich has escaped from a farm for criminal ostriches and is still at large. 'He was the only one living on the farm and I can't find him anywhere,' said the Ostrich Farm Keeper. 'He must have escaped!'

Police have warned people not to approach the ostrich, which has a long history of headbutting letterboxes, stomping on squirrels and biting anything within reach. Police said the bird's full name was **STRUTHIO OSTRICH** and could be identified by its 'long neck, long legs and fluffy middle bit'.

The ostrich sounds terrifying. Rock knows this is a job for the **REAL PIGEONS**.

Then the most unexpected thing happens.

Rock doesn't understand.

He isn't looking forward to meeting Struthio Ostrich. But is this mission really *too dangerous*?

'PLEASE!' begs the mouse.

'We already have to worry about being eaten by cats and owls and hawks,' says the lizard. 'Now there's a **DANGEROUS OSTRICH** too!'

'I'M TASTY!'

'I'M ALSO TASTY!'

Rock doesn't know what to do.
Grandpouter has said two different things.

'Crime-fighters should **HELP CREATURES IN NEED.**'

'**OSTRICHES ARE TOO DANGEROUS.**'

Which Grandpouter is right?

Rock decides that what really matters is helping the creatures. 'We'll just have to be careful,' he says.

'Take the case if you want. But I don't recommend it.'

The other **REAL PIGEONS** agree with Rock.

'**REAL PIGEONS CATCH OSTRICHES!**'

cry all the pigeons (except Grandpouter).

GULP!

'Now we can relax!'

'Let's google photos of sandcastles and pretend we're at the beach!'

PIGEONS are
REAL
FRIENDS
REAL

The pigeons start looking for the escaped ostrich.

unhappy

nervous

Ostriches are as tall as humans. And Struthio Ostrich is a **DANGEROUS CRIMINAL** that bites!

Rock was expecting to find a **TRAIL OF DESTRUCTION** in the streets. But strangely, there are no signs of the ostrich anywhere.

'These flowers have **NOT** been stomped on.'

'This street sign is **NOT** bent over.'

'These rocks have NOT been eaten,' says Grandpouter.

'Huh?'

'Ostriches eat rocks,' says Grandpouter.

'It helps them digest food. It's a fact.'

Grandpouter is acting so strangely.

'Why don't you want to catch the ostrich?' asks Rock.

Grandpouter ruffles his feathers.

ruffle
ruffle

'I just think we should train more as a squad first,' he says.

'We haven't even **EATEN DANGER** yet.'

'We can't find the ostrich anyway,' says Frillback.

'Let's go to the **OSTRICH FARM**,' says Homey. 'Maybe we can find clues about where he went?'

OSTRICH FARM

Let's keep them where we can see them!

The pigeons fly to the Ostrich Farm. It isn't like the farm Rock once lived on.

TUMBLEWEED FACTORY

TUMBLEWEED FACTORY

swirly barbed wire!

unclimbable fence

more barbed wire!

water tank

for tools

BEWARE: OSTRICH HAS NAUGHTY IDEAS AND A BAD TEMPER.

OSTRICH FARM

ALSO, HE BITES.

88

'Struthio Ostrich does **NOT** sound friendly,' says Tumbler.

'We could just go home?' suggests Grandpouter.

'Or we could visit that garden down there for a snack instead?' suggests Homey.

snacks!

so many snacks!

Skinny Latte CAFE

89

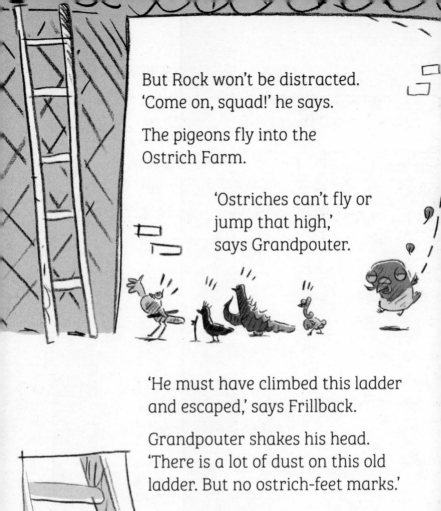

But Rock won't be distracted.
'Come on, squad!' he says.

The pigeons fly into the
Ostrich Farm.

'Ostriches can't fly or
jump that high,'
says Grandpouter.

'He must have climbed this ladder
and escaped,' says Frillback.

Grandpouter shakes his head.
'There is a lot of dust on this old
ladder. But no ostrich-feet marks.'

Rock is puzzled.
'If Struthio Ostrich
didn't use the ladder,
HOW did he get out?'

IT'S A TOTAL MYSTERY!

There are no holes in the fences.

No broken doors or windows.

No lion statues leading to secret underground places.

Rock twitches his toes nervously. 'Perhaps the ostrich hasn't escaped at all,' he says. 'Maybe he's still here!'

The pigeons all gulp as they look at the big pile of leaves in the middle of the farm.

ostrich??

'We should get out of here,' says Grandpouter.

'No,' says Frillback. 'I'll take care of this.'

She marches forward bravely, and leaps into the leaves.

'He's not in here!' says Frillback.

92

CHAPTER 2

Struthio Ostrich is

SNAP-SNAP-SNAPPING

at the pigeons.

He looks like a snake wrestling a feather duster. Utterly terrifying!

The **REAL PIGEONS** are **REAL SCARED**. But they can't run away. They have to **work together as a team**.

'We have to catch that ostrich!' Rock says.

'Or not.'

But Struthio Ostrich isn't worried by a few pigeons.

He kicks Homey off his toenails.

Ties a knot in the middle of Tumbler.

Headbutts Frillback away.

And **GOBBLES UP ROCK!**

'How dare you **EAT ROCK!**' cries Frillback. 'Spit him out at once!'

'**WRONG ROCK,**' laughs Struthio. '**TASTES BAD!**'

Before the pigeons have a chance to recover, Struthio scoops them into a butterfly net.

'Oh dear!'

'PIGEONS TRAPPED!' says Struthio Ostrich.

'STRUTHIO WINNER!'

THE PIGEONS GASP.

'You pretended to escape from the farm just so you could trap us!' says Rock.

Struthio Ostrich nods. **'WE PLANNED – PIGEONS CAME!'**

'Now would be a good time to **EAT DANGER**,' says Grandpouter. 'Or at least chew a hole in this net.'

Rock is wondering *why* the ostrich laid this trap when he hears the gate clatter.

'Stop right there, Struthio!' says the human. 'I thought you'd escaped!'

Struthio ditches the pigeons and says:

'NOT OVER – SWORN ENEMY!'

With that, the ostrich takes off . . .

darts around the human . . .

'DANG!'

and escapes.

For real, this time.

'I'm his **SWORN ENEMY**? How did that happen?' says Rock.

The human runs out on to the street.

And the pigeons take to the skies.

'Where did he go?'

'That ostrich is FAST!'

'**HELP!**
HAS ANYONE SEEN
AN EVIL OSTRICH?'

But Struthio Ostrich
is nowhere to be seen.

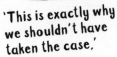

'This is exactly why
we shouldn't have
taken the case,' says Grandpouter.

Rock wonders if Grandpouter
was right. Maybe the
ostrich *is* too dangerous.

But why was Struthio trying to
trap them? And why does he think
Rock is his **SWORN ENEMY?**

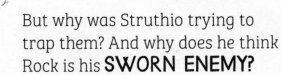

The **REAL PIGEONS** land on the street again.

'I couldn't EAT DANGER!'

'The DANGER ate me!'

'My tummy is literally in knots!'

The ostrich didn't trap them. But he has left them in a sorry state.

Rock is not giving up, though. 'We've got to find Struthio Ostrich again,' he cries.

Homey shrugs. 'There's a little garden near the farm. He could be hiding in there?'

Rock throws a wing around Homey.

'That's the spirit. Let's go investigate!'

Homey is a homing pigeon. He knows how to fly anywhere in the world. But there's another reason he wants to visit the garden.

Homey wanted breadcrumbs.

'I'll make it easy for you, dude.'

'Do you ever use your **PIGEON POWERS** to actually fight crime?' says Frillback.

'You can't fight crime on an empty tummy, PIG,' replies Homey.

'I'm going to teach you a lesson, **PIG!**' cries Frillback.

She jumps on Homey and they start fighting.

Again.

Rock sits down on a rock.
He doesn't know what to do.

'This knot is giving
me a tummy ache.'

The other pigeons have lost interest
in catching Struthio Ostrich.

Rock looks at his twig.

'It's just you
and me, Trent,' he says.

'Do you still want
to fight crime?'

Rock looks up, and sees something at the top of a nearby tower block.

The fluffy middle part of an ostrich.

'Struthio Ostrich!'

TUMBLEWEED FACTORY

Rock starts to feel hopeful.

Maybe, if they work as a team, they can still catch the ostrich.

And Rock will find out why Struthio called him his '**SWORN ENEMY**'.

So he unpicks Tumbler's knot.

Separates Frillback and Homey.

'Trent says no fighting.'

And rallies the pigeons.

'I just saw Struthio up there on a rooftop. Will you help me, REAL PIGEONS? Or should I say: REAL FRIENDS?'

They follow Rock to the rooftop.

'I REALLY think we should leave this case alone, squad!'

But when they arrive, the ostrich isn't there.

Although something else is.

'Is that a **giant breadcrumb?**' says Homey.

'**WOW!**'

The giant breadcrumb is **marvellous**.

clean undies (not food!)

REJECTS

not food

FOOD!

tumbleweed (not food!)

'It's the most beautiful thing I've ever seen,' says Homey.

'I hate to agree with Homey.'

says Frillback.

'But I agree with Homey.'

Rock wants to eat the breadcrumb.
And dance with it. And hug it.

Until he starts thinking.
'Something's not quite right.'

'How did a giant breadcrumb get up here?'
says Rock. 'Breadcrumbs can't fly.'

But the others brush past him.

'A quick bite won't hurt,' says Tumbler.
'We deserve a treat after getting our feathery
behinds kicked by the ostrich!'

They sink their beaks into the breadcrumb.

And a shadow appears overhead.

CHAPTER 3

Rock sees the shadow and darts away – right before a

BIG CAGE SLAMS DOWN.

Struthio Ostrich stands there proudly.

The giant breadcrumb was bait.

The pigeons have fallen right into Struthio's trap.

AGAIN.

Luckily, Struthio hasn't seen Rock yet.

So Rock quickly flies up
to a nearby washing line.

He has never hidden in underwear
before. It's not the kind of costume
a **MASTER OF DISGUISE** usually
wears. But right now Rock has
no choice.

tumble
tumble

Struthio Ostrich jumps on top of the cage and looks in with a sneer.

'STRUTHIO **SMART** —
PIGEONS
DUMB!'

tumble
tumble

'**Look on the bright side, dudes – at least we won't go hungry!'** says Homey.

Rock needs to rescue the others.

But how is he going to get over there without being seen?

'Of course!' he whispers. 'I just need to blend in!'

Rock dives into
a tumbleweed,

SMACK!

rolls across the roof . . .

. . . and arrives at the cage.

REJECTS

'Psst! **SQUAD!**' he says in a low voice.
'It's me. I've come to save you!'

'Nice disguise, **PIG**!' says Homey.

'I totally thought you were
a tumbleweed. Here, have some
of the giant breadcrumb!'

munch!

munch!

'Save yourself, Rock –
while you still can!'
says Grandpouter.

113

'Don't tell Rock to leave!' cries Frillback.
'We need him, Grandpouter.'

'Grandpouter Pigeon?' mumbles Struthio,
who is settling down for a nap.

'SWORN ENEMY!'

Suddenly, Rock understands.

'I'm not Struthio's **SWORN ENEMY**,' whispers Rock. 'Grandpouter is. You know this ostrich, don't you?'

Grandpouter nods sadly.

On top of the cage, Struthio is snoring. He has fallen asleep.

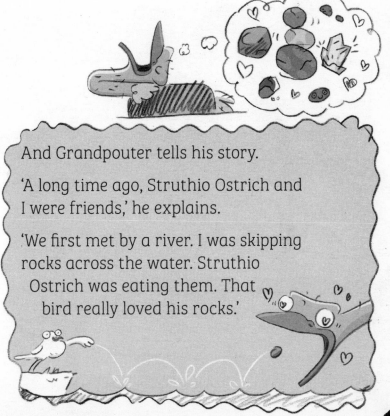

And Grandpouter tells his story.

'A long time ago, Struthio Ostrich and I were friends,' he explains.

'We first met by a river. I was skipping rocks across the water. Struthio Ostrich was eating them. That bird really loved his rocks.'

'A thief struck nearby,' remembers Grandpouter.

'Stop! Thief!'

'Struthio and I didn't waste a second. We joined forces and caught the thief.

'Thanks, bird heroes!'

'We became instant best friends – and crime-fighting partners.

'We caught lots of bad guys. Until the day we came across a pet-rock shop. Struthio couldn't help himself.

'I should have calmed Stuthio down. But instead, I fetched the police. Struthio flew into a temper. He went on a biting rampage. The police took him to the Ostrich Farm. But Struthio blamed me.'

Back in the cage, a tear rolls down Rock's beak. Grandpouter's story is so sad. No wonder he has been acting strangely.

'I think Struthio has trapped us as revenge,' says Grandpouter, taking a deep breath. 'So I should put an end to this. **STRUTHIO!**'

The ostrich wakes up.

'Why don't you let the other pigeons go?' says Grandpouter. 'It's just me you want.'

Struthio shakes his head.

'ENJOY CAGE – SWORN ENEMY.'

Then he says something that puts fear into the pigeons' hearts.

'WHAT'S NEXT – FAR WORSE!'

There is no time to waste.

Rock needs to break the pigeons out of that cage. And fast!

He rolls across to the edge of the roof and leaps out of his tumbleweed disguise.

He has an idea for how to rescue his friends. But first he'll have to visit someone.

Someone who isn't exactly a friend.

TUMBLEWEED
FACTORY

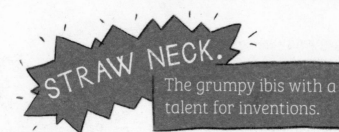

STRAW NECK.

The grumpy ibis with a talent for inventions.

'Let me gets this straight – you need a long pink sock?'

'Yes.'

'To help with a case?'

'That's right.'

'You can't fight crime without a long pink sock?'

'Not today.'

'I honestly don't understand why everyone thinks **REAL PIGEONS** are such great crime-fighters.'

'Do you have a sock or not?'

'Uhh. Yes. Hang on and I'll get it.'

'Thanks. I also need a shoelace and some newspaper.'

Straw Neck gives everything to Rock.

'Thanks,' says Rock.

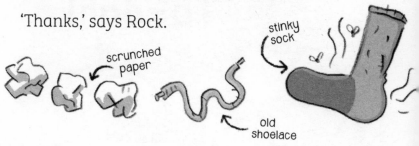

scrunched paper

stinky sock

old shoelace

He sews the shoelace on to the sock. Then he fills it with scrunched-up newspaper.

'I WAS going to invent a sleeping bag for snakes with that sock!'

Pigeons are too small to dress up as ostriches.

Instead, Rock has made a puppet.

A STRUTHIO OSTRICH PUPPET!

'Ta-dah!'

'A snake will go cold tonight because of you.'

Rock flies away.

The **REAL PIGEONS** couldn't catch Struthio Ostrich.

But according to Grandpouter, the police caught him once before.

Rock hopes they can do it again.

'Hey, Jack, isn't that Struthio Ostrich?'

'Yeah, he escaped from the farm. We'd better catch him.'

CHAPTER 4

Struthio slams the door shut so the police can't get in. Then he seizes Rock and takes the other pigeons out of the cage.

'Straw Neck!' shouts Rock. 'What's going on?'

BANG
BANG
BANG

'Birdo, I'm going to tell you straight,' says Straw Neck with a snarl. 'Your crime-fighting days are **OVER!**'

'*I'm* taking over the crime-fighting around here,' says Straw Neck, 'because you pigeons are *not* good at it. You never would have freed the bottled birds without me. And now Struthio and I have lured you into *two* traps!'

Straw Neck throws some rocks to the ostrich, who gobbles them greedily.

'Good boy, Struthio! We did it!'

'**WE PLANNED,**' says the ostrich, as he swallows rocks. '**PIGEON TRAPS!**'

'So *you're* the one who helped Struthio set that trap at the Ostrich Farm!' cries Rock. 'But why??'

'They'll think you've climbed this ladder and already escaped.'

'I recognised Grandpouter from when he and Struthio used to be a team,' says Straw Neck. 'Now I've brought them back together. Because part of my deal with Struthio is that . . . he gets to keep Grandpouter.'

'SWORN ENEMY – YOU MINE!'

'And what are you going to do with the rest of us?' says Rock.

'I'm going to break up the **REAL PIGEONS** squad – forever,' laughs Straw Neck. 'By taking each of you to a different corner of the world and leaving you there. You'll never see each other again. And I'll be free to fight crime here on my own.'

THE PIGEONS SHUDDER IN HORROR.

'Although we'll leave Homey here in this cage, because he's a homing pigeon,'

says Straw Neck.

'We don't want him flying back and bringing you all along.'

Rock never liked Straw Neck much.

But he didn't think she'd do something this **terrible**.

'You can't be a crime-fighter if you do bad things like separate a squad of friends!' cries Rock.

Straw Neck smiles with her crooked beak. 'You forget my motto, Rock – sometimes you have to be **BAD** to be **GOOD!**'

But someone shouts behind them.

'A better motto is –
**REAL PIGEONS
EAT DANGER!**'

'ARGH!'

screams Struthio.

The ostrich feathers
that were holding
Grandpouter are gone.

'Grandpouter has
EATEN DANGER!
And escaped!'
Rock shouts.

'COO!'

'EW!'

132

'HEY STRUTHIO!' shouts Grandpouter. 'YOU'RE NOT MY SWORN ENEMY! YOU'RE JUST A BAD BIRD!'

The ostrich spins around, and Grandpouter clobbers him over the head with Straw Neck's scooter.

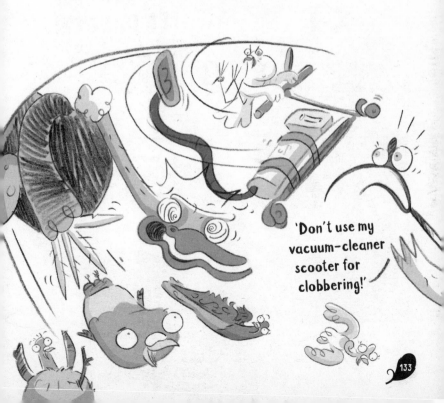

'Don't use my vacuum-cleaner scooter for clobbering!'

The police officers finally burst through the door.

'There's the criminal ostrich!'

'Catch him!'

Straw Neck hides behind the cage while the police officers try to handcuff Struthio.

But there's a problem.

'These won't fit an ostrich!'

says one of the police officers.

Luckily, Rock knows what to do.

He takes back all the **REAL PIGEONS'** friendship bands . . .

. . . and ties them into one long **STRINGY THING.**

Then he throws it to the police. Who use it as a leash.

'Thanks, tumbleweed bird!'

'I'm glad you took the case,' says Grandpouter to Rock. 'I've been scared of Struthio Ostrich for years. But now I'm free!'

'Thanks!'

'BYE!'

'Hooray!' cries Rock.

'We caught the ostrich and everything is good again!'

But then Grandpouter faints.

Rock gasps.

'Grandpouter! Are you OK?'

Straw Neck snatches back her vacuum-cleaner scooter. 'Oh, didn't I mention, birdo? I put a sleeping potion in that giant breadcrumb! It takes a while to kick in, but it's **VERY** powerful.'

'Oh no!' cries Rock. 'We have all **EATEN DANGER** – in the worst possible way!' Frillback and Tumbler fall asleep too.

'All of you pigeons will be asleep soon,' says Straw Neck.

'HE HE HE HE HE HE!'

Then Rock and Homey fall asleep.

A number of hours later, the pigeons wake up.

They are upside down.

And being flown through the air.

Straw Neck drops them off.
One by one. Just like she said she would.

She drops Tumbler off
on top of Mount Everest.
Where it is **cold** and **lonely**.

'NOOOOOOOO!'

She drops Frillback in the middle of the desert.

Where it is **hot** and **lonely**.

'NOOOOOOOO!'

She drops Grandpouter in the middle of a Brazilian street party.

Where it is **crowded** and **lonely**.

'NOOOOOOOO!'

And finally, Straw Neck drops Rock on an island in the middle of the ocean.

Where it is **lonely** and **lonely**.

The **REAL PIGEONS** have never been further apart.

Will they ever see each other again?

Will they ever fight crime again?

THE END . . . FOR NOW

OH MY GOSLING!

THIS IS STRESSFUL!

At least the lizard and mouse are safe now.

'Hey, I heard that ostrich was caught.'

'Good, I can go back to sunbathing in public.'

142

BUT PLEASE KEEP READING.

WE CAN'T LEAVE THE REAL PIGEONS LIKE THIS.

WE JUST CAN'T.

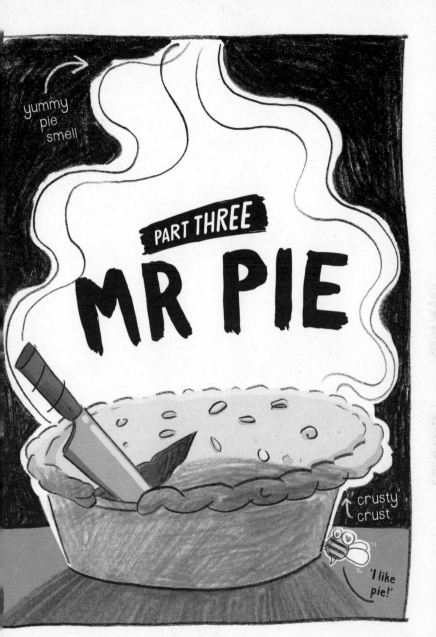

CHAPTER 1

There are no crime-fighting pigeons in the city.

Not since they went missing.

However, a certain ibis is ready to take on the crime-fighting.

'A real ibis doesn't just invent things. **A REAL IBIS FIGHTS CRIME!**'

'I love that cape!'

'Very dashing!'

Straw Neck sees her first crime unfolding.

Some kids are kicking a ball . . .

. . . in a park where ball games are not allowed.

THIS IS A JOB FOR STRAW NECK!

She quickly stops the game.

'Sorry, kiddos. I have no choice but to stop this crime.'

PFFFFFFFF!

Then she sees two ducks fighting
over a hamburger.

This situation could get out of control.

So Straw Neck jumps in.

'**Hey!**'

'Sorry, duckos.
I have no choice but
to eat this crime.'

The problem is gone.
So is the hamburger.

Then Straw Neck sees
a boy climbing a tree.

'These birds are squawking a lot. Maybe they need help?'

VROOOOM!!!

Some blackbirds are in danger.

Luckily, Straw Neck isn't just a crime-fighting ibis. She's an inventor too.

151

She takes a remote from her belt.
It controls one of her best inventions.

A DRONE WINDOW WASHER

wet mop

whirly blades

drone

Straw Neck flies the Drone Window Washer up into the tree . . .

... and pushes
the boy out.

'My arm!'

'Oh no!'

Straw Neck has saved the blackbirds.

But she has hurt the boy.

Every time Straw Neck does
a **GOOD THING**,
she also does a
BAD THING.

But as she is flying off, the blackbirds call out.
'Help! Please help us!'

'Our babies are missing!' cries the mother
blackbird. 'We don't know where they've gone!'

'Fear not, blackbirdos,' says Straw Neck.

'I WILL SAVE THEM!'

Uh-oh. If only the
blackbirds knew what
she was **really** like.

MEANWHILE, IN FOUR DIFFERENT CORNERS OF THE WORLD . . .

The **REAL PIGEONS** are all miserable and far from home.

All except one.

Our last heroic pigeon finally wakes up.

TUMBLEWEED FACTORY

He is in the big wooden cage on the rooftop where Straw Neck and Struthio Ostrich trapped the **REAL PIGEONS**.

'How long have I been out for?'

He remembers **EVERYTHING**.

Straw Neck wanted to leave Homey behind because he is a **homing pigeon**.

Homing pigeons know how to fly anywhere in the world – and back again.

Straw Neck couldn't risk Homey flying back home with all the pigeons.

But even though he's locked up, the remaining **REAL PIGEON** smiles to himself.

Because there is one thing Straw Neck didn't count on.

THIS ISN'T HOMEY!

'SURPRISE!'

It's Rock Pigeon. All this time he has been in disguise, *pretending* to be Homey!

Meanwhile, on an island in the middle of the ocean, another pigeon takes off his tumbleweed disguise.

But it's not Rock – it's Homey.

'SURPRISE... DUDES!'

The two pigeons have switched places. But how did they do it?

It was Rock's idea.

Before Straw Neck took most of the pigeons away, Homey put on Rock's tumbleweed costume.

'All you pigeons will be asleep soon. HE HE HE –

-HE HE HE!'

And Rock used a slice of bread to dress up like Homey.

They switched places so Homey could fly back home. And pick up Frillback, Tumbler and Grandpouter on the way.

The real Homey takes off.

It's time for him to use his **PIGEON POWER**.

He must find the others and get home as quickly as possible.

But then he sees a boat full of breadsticks...

'You can't be a hero on an empty tummy!'

HMS BREADSTICK

Will Homey ever make it home?

CHAPTER 2

Back in the cage, Rock is feeling lonely.

He hopes Homey will return soon with the squad. They need to stop Straw Neck before she does any more damage!

But how can he catch her without the other **REAL PIGEONS** to help him?

He decides he has to try. At least he still has Trent.

First, they need to get out of the cage.

So Rock plucks a few feathers from
his neck ...

... and sticks them
to Trent.

Who is now disguised
as a colourful flower.

Eventually a bee appears.

Because bees love colourful flowers.

'Hello bee!'
says Rock.

'Can you please lift
this cage off me?'

163

'**Zilly pigeon!**'
says the bee.

'Beez do not do favourz.
We only do bizznezz.
Hey, thiz flower iz not real!'

The bee looks cross. And when bees are cross,
they sting. So, Rock tries some **bizznezz**.

'Would you like
a new hive?' he says.

'This ... er ... box
would be perfect for
making honey in.'

The bee thinks for a moment.

— 'Yezzz. **OK!**'

The bee gets his friends
and they carry the
cage away.

'A pleazure doing
bizznezz with
you, pigeon!'

Finally, Rock and Trent are free.

'Letz do thiz! Eh, I mean – **let's do this!'**
says Rock.

Trent remains silent. Having a twig isn't quite the same as having **REAL** friends.

'Where are the **REAL PIGEONS?**' wonders Rock. 'They should have been back by now.'

But he tries not to worry. Because the time has come to track down Straw Neck.

Rock starts looking and notices some sad faces.

'The ibis did it!'

It seems like Straw Neck has been this way.

'Why would an ibis steal our food?'

'I swear, a Drone Window Washer pushed me out of that tree.'

Rock flies up into the tree to investigate ...

. . . where he comes face-to-face with the ibis.

'Oh my gosling!'
says Straw Neck.

'Rock Pigeon?
That's impossible!'

'Straw Neck!' cries Rock. 'Are you doing
something **BAD** again?'

'**No!**' shouts Straw Neck.

'I'm doing something
GOOD again!'

'Who are you?'
says the mother
blackbird to Rock.

But Rock and Straw Neck keep arguing.

'I fight the crime these days, birdo. And I do it ALONE!'

'Well, I prefer to work with my squad – which *someone* took to the far corners of the world!'

'How did you get all the way back from that island?' cries Straw Neck.

'You took the wrong pigeon!' snaps Rock.

'EXCUSE ME!'

cries one of the blackbirds.

'Is anybody going to help find our missing babies?'

'Your babies are missing?' says Rock.

'Yes, we have ten babies,' says the father.

'But when we woke up this morning, the nest was empty.'

'We checked, and our babies didn't fall out,' says the mother.

'So they must have been stolen!'

Who would **birdnap** baby blackbirds?

'Don't worry – I'll find them!' says Rock.

'Not if I find them first!' sneers Straw Neck.

And the ibis flies off.

Rock speeds after Straw Neck.

It's a race to save the baby blackbirds.

'Let's make a deal,' says Straw Neck. 'If I save the blackbirds, you have to let me be this city's **ONLY** crime-fighter.'

'But if I find them first,' says Rock, '**you** have to go fetch Homey, Tumbler, Frillback and Grandpouter and bring them all home.'

Rock knows he can't trust Straw Neck. So he shouldn't make a deal. But he misses his friends. He wants them back.

'**Deal?**'
asks Straw Neck.

'**Deal!**'
Rock says.

Grey clouds gather as Rock and Straw Neck continue their frantic search.

SPECIALITY PIES
from the
Prince of Pastry
and the **King of Crust** –
MR PIE!

BILL BIRD'S BILLBOARDS

'I know you think I'm the most terrible bird ever,' says Straw Neck. 'But trust me – there are far worse birds out there.'

Rock doesn't believe it. 'Like *who*?'

'**Vultures**,'
says Straw Neck.

'You'd better flee if you ever meet a vulture. They are **OMENS OF DOOM!** They eat bones and will **CURSE** you with a lifetime of bad luck.'

'**I don't believe you**,' says Rock.

Straw Neck shrugs. 'I'm just saying – I'm not as bad as you think I am.'

Raindrops start to fall. At that moment, they both spot something on the ground.

'Blackbird feathers!'

They land on the street. The trail of feathers stops outside a building.

'The baby blackbirds must be inside,' says Rock. 'How are we going to get in?'

Straw Neck picks up a big rock.

'I'll break the window, then fly through the hole.'

'Don't you see?' cries Rock.

'Throwing a rock through a window is **BAD**.'

'But saving babies is

GOOD,'

says Straw Neck. She throws the rock.

SMASH!

A loud voice booms out of the restaurant.

'WHOEVER THREW THAT ROCK, I'M COMING TO GET YOU!'

'Oh no!' cries Straw Neck. 'What now?'

Rock suddenly realises it's not just the blackbirds he needs to save. He needs to save Straw Neck, too. He needs to stop her doing **BAD THINGS** before she gets worse. Before she turns out like Struthio Ostrich!

'Quick!' says Rock. 'Let's hide!'

Rock borrows Straw Neck's cape.

He pulls out Trent and collects some other sticks too.

'What are you doing?'
　　　cries Straw Neck.

'We should get out of here!'

'I have a better idea,'
says Rock.

'Get into this
thing with me!'

Rock has made a clever disguise:
an umbrella.

Thunder claps in the sky above.

Rain pours down.

The restaurant door flies open.

'There's no-one out here!'

'Just an old umbrella.'

'It might be useful if this rain keeps up.'

Rock's disguise hasn't just hidden them.

It's got them into the restaurant, too!

Rock and Straw Neck
are put in an umbrella
stand inside the
restaurant.

'Your disguise
worked, birdo!'

Rock is surprised to see the nice man from
the park here.

'Ladies and gentlemen,
welcome to my restaurant,'
says the man.
'I am Mr Pie!
The Prince of Pastry and
the King of Crust!'

But where are the baby blackbirds?

'Tonight we will be serving a rare treat,' says Mr Pie.

'BABY BLACKBIRD PIE!'

'Oh, no!'

Mr Pie is not a nice man after all. He's been feeding birds in the park to fatten them up! How cruel!

'I'm scared,' says Rock.

'Me too, birdo,' says Straw Neck.

But things are about to get scarier.

'Let's celebrate our feast with champagne!'
cries Mr Pie.

POP!

A lady grabs an umbrella to shield herself
from the shower.

AND ROCK AND STRAW NECK
TUMBLE OUT!

The chef grabs Rock and Straw Neck.

'I know you!'

She is the same woman who tried to buy bottled birds from Goldpinch!

Mr Pie's eyes get bulgy. His smile grows too big.

'Good news!' he announces.

'Some fresh ingredients have just flown in. Let's add a **PIGEON AND IBIS PIE** to the menu!'

'NOOOOOOO!'

CHAPTER 3

Rock and Straw Neck are taken into the kitchen, where the chef washes them . . .

and pegs them up to dry . . .

'This is not what a **STRINGY THING** is for!'

... with the baby blackbirds.
Luckily, they haven't been baked yet.

'Now we're all **DOOMED**,' says Straw Neck. 'I don't want to be a crime-fighter any more.'

The birds wriggle, kick and do sad faces.

SAD → SADDER → SADDEST

But the chef laughs at them. 'I can't wait to **pluck**, **chop** and **bake** you in a pie!' she says. 'Then I will eat you, lick my lips and pick my teeth with this twig I found!'

'Trent! No!'

'Trent's not a toothpick!'

The chef leaves the kitchen to pick some herbs from the garden.

The birds are in deep trouble now.

Rock dearly wishes the **REAL PIGEONS** were here. They always work best as a team.

That word sticks in his head – **team**.

'The deal we made is stupid,' Rock says to Straw Neck.

'We should have been working as a team. Because – I admit – you're nowhere near as bad as Mr Pie.'

'Or as bad as a vulture,' says Straw Neck.

'I'm sorry I kidnapped the **REAL PIGEONS** and spread them out across the world. But the good news is, I know how we can get out of here.'

Rock gasps. 'Really? How?'

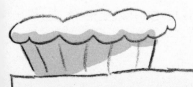

185

'I have just invented an escape plan,' says Straw Neck, proudly. 'I invented it in my head.'

'So how do we escape?' asks Rock.

'Simple,' says Straw Neck. 'We all hold feet.'

Straw Neck points to a lamp on the edge of the cupboard and explains her plan.

'You might be a **BAD** crime-fighter, but you're a **GOOD** inventor,' says Rock.

Straw Neck gets all the birds to swing back and forth, until they go so high they knock the cupboard. The lamp on the edge moves closer and closer.

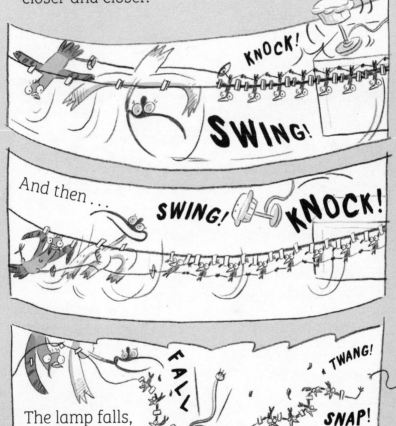

And then...

The lamp falls, snapping the line in two.

The birds unpeg each other
and run for the open window.

They have almost all escaped . . .

'Let go of me,
STRINGY THING!'

. . . when Rock gets tangled up in the rope.

All the birds are out of
the window now.

Except for Rock
and Straw Neck.

Rock grabs Straw Neck's wing, just as the chef returns. 'Please don't leave me here,' begs Rock. 'I know you're a **GOOD** bird at heart!'

'Sorry, Rock,' says Straw Neck. 'Even **GOOD** birdos do **BAD** things sometimes.'

The ibis shakes him off and leaps out the of window.

'**Nooooo!**'

Straw Neck and the baby blackbirds fly off.

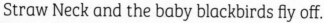

'You'd better be a tasty pigeon,' growls the chef,

'because you just became the **MAIN COURSE!'**

She grabs Rock and puts rubber bands around him. Then takes him back to the dining room.

'**I must apologise,**' says Mr Pie to his guests.

'After our starter, tonight's meal will now just be **PIGEON PIE.'**

'It will be prepared in front of you to stop any more escape attempts!' adds the chef.

She holds up a knife.

Rock looks away. He sees something moving in the dark hallway. A shape appears and Rock gasps.

It's just a waiter with a hunch and a beaky nose. He's bringing in the starters.

Rock shakes his head.

He shouldn't believe anything Straw Neck has told him. That lousy traitor!

Rock tries to remain hopeful.

But it's almost impossible.

He's lost his squad.

He's lost his twig.

Straw Neck has abandoned him.

Now he's all alone.

Rock is feeling so low that he doesn't notice some food wobbling in front of him. Until . . .

... the **REAL PIGEONS** burst out!

They were hiding in the food!

'REAL PIGEONS FOOD FIGHT!'

Rock smiles the biggest smile you've ever seen.

SO BIG!

Straw Neck appears too. The restaurant is thrown into chaos as the birds battle the humans.

SQUIRT!

FRISBEE!

It has been a dirty fight. There is food everywhere. The humans flee.

'FLEE!'

'I've had it with birds. From now on, I only cook vegetarian!'

'No, please don't leave!'

'ESCAPE!'

Rock is saved and the **REAL PIGEONS** are reunited.

'How did you know where I was?' cries Rock.

'After I took the baby blackbirds back to their parents, I found the **REAL PIGEONS** in the park,' says Straw Neck.
'They were looking for you.'

'Thanks hero!'

'First Straw Neck kidnaps us. Then she helps us. Weird bird!'

Just then, Mr Pie sees Frillback trying to free Rock.

'I lost all my customers because of **YOU**,' Mr Pie yells at Rock.

'You deserve to bake RIGHT NOW! Feathers and all!'

Mr Pie grabs Rock and shoves him into a pie case.

'HELP!'

Then he sticks pastry over the top . . .

. . . and slides him into the hot oven.

Where Rock begins to roast.

Mr Pie blocks the oven.

'I KNOW WHAT I WANT TO EAT TONIGHT!'

he shouts.

'Poor Rock!'

'He'll be cooked to a crisp!'

But there is one thing Mr Pie doesn't know.

A twig can be a **SECRET WEAPON.**

'TWIG TORPEDO!'

Frillback rams Mr Pie with her giant twig and pins him against the wall.

'I thought this might come in handy again.'

Then she uses a chair to hold him in place.

'Goo goo, ga ga?'

'You don't look too good, Mr Pie. Have a seat!'

Homey and Tumbler find some oven-proof active wear.

And retrieve the pie.

But are they too late?

'Oh no.'

They put the pie on the table.

It is hot and black.

'I can't bear to look inside,' says Grandpouter.

'**Poor Rock**,' says Straw Neck, sadly.

'**A vulture must have visited him and cursed him!**'

'**Maybe Rock never went into the pie**,' says Homey hopefully. '**Maybe he did another switch!**'

Homey grabs random objects, hoping they are Rock in disguise.

'Rock, is that you?'

'Are you in here, Rock?'

'Rock? Tell me this is your amazing fork costume?'

But those things are not Rock.

'Sorry to interrupt,' says a voice from the doorway. 'But are you looking for me?'

'IT'S ROCK! HOORAY!'

'Rock, you are an **incredible** pigeon,' says Grandpouter. 'How did you escape from the oven?'

Rock laughs. 'It turns out the oven has a chimney,' says Rock.

'As soon as I was in the oven, I slipped out of the pie and flew up to the roof.'

HOW ROCK ESCAPED

↑ to the roof

evil bird eater!

door

pie

fire

crackle crackle

'**Amazing!**' says Frillback. 'You rescued yourself!'

But Rock knows who **REALLY** rescued him.

'Thanks for saving me, **REAL PIGEONS!**' he says. 'I'm so glad you found your way home.'

HMS BREADSTICK

'We got a little distracted on the way,' says Homey. 'But we were always coming for you!'

'The truth is that we couldn't have saved you without Straw Neck,' says Grandpouter.

Rock is strangely proud of Straw Neck.

'You did **GOOD**, birdo,' grins Rock.

'Sorry I had to leave,' says Straw Neck. 'I knew I could come back once the babies were safe. But fighting crime is too dangerous. So I've decided to go back to inventing things. Let me know if you need anything invented, birdo!'

'Thanks, Straw Necko,' says Rock.

Rock has saved Straw Neck from becoming a villain. **HOORAY!**

The **REAL PIGEONS** leave the restaurant. On the way, Rock finds his twig on the ground.

'Long time no see, Trent!'

Mr Pie is still trapped inside when a swarm of bees flies past.

'Let's make this old building our new home,' say the bees.

'We need a big space now that we have such a large hive.'

'Nooooo, I hate bees!'

BUzzzzzz

And Mr Pie's screams can be heard for miles.

'Nooooooooo!'

Meanwhile, the **REAL PIGEONS** head for home. They are tired, but happy to be together again.

'I'm going to make new friendship bands,' announces Rock, as they fly.

'We can all help with that,' smiles Grandpouter.

Soon, the pigeons (and Trent) are back on their gazebo roof and weaving.

BECAUSE THEY ARE ALL REAL **FRIENDS.**

THE END

HOWEVER...

THE REAL PIGEONS
AREN'T ALONE.

Little do they know
they're about to meet...

DID YOU KNOW

REAL PIGEONS

ARE

REAL-LIFE PIGEONS?

ROCK PIGEON

The most common pigeon in the world. Grey with two black stripes on each wing. Very good at blending in!

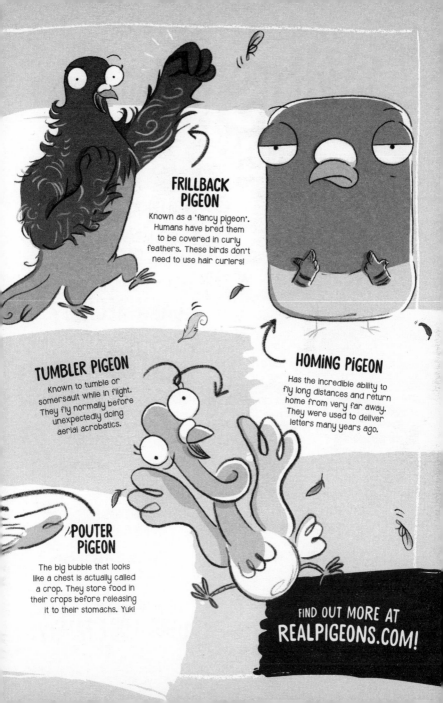

FRILLBACK PIGEON

Known as a 'fancy pigeon'. Humans have bred them to be covered in curly feathers. These birds don't need to use hair curlers!

HOMING PIGEON

Has the incredible ability to fly long distances and return home from very far away. They were used to deliver letters many years ago.

TUMBLER PIGEON

Known to tumble or somersault while in flight. They fly normally before unexpectedly doing aerial acrobatics.

POUTER PIGEON

The big bubble that looks like a chest is actually called a crop. They store food in their crops before releasing it to their stomachs. Yuk!

FIND OUT MORE AT REALPIGEONS.COM!

HAVE YOU READ ALL THE REAL PIGEONS' ADVENTURES? NO?

WHAT ARE YOU WAITING FOR, YOUR FEATHERS TO GROW?

BOOK TWO

A series of mysteries threatens to tear apart the pigeon squad:

WHO IS BOTTLING BIRDS?

HOW DID A DERANGED OSTRICH ESCAPE HIS OSTRICH FARM?

AND WHAT IS THE PIE MAKER'S DARK SECRET?

BOOK THREE

Rock wants to make a perfect nest for the squad, but investigations keep getting in the way:

BOOK ONE

Rock and his mystery-solving pigeon pals tackle their first caseload:

WHY HAVE ALL THE BREADCRUMBS DISAPPEARED?

WHO ON EARTH IS KIDNAPPING BATS?

AND CAN THEY AVERT A DINNER DISASTER??

WHO HAS STOLEN A VULTURE'S NEST?

HOW DID A BEASTLY CHILD GET LOST IN A PARK?

AND WILL HOMEY EVER FIND HIS LONG-LOST FAMILY?

The pigeons need to keep their beaks above water as they look into some splashy mysteries:

BOOK FOUR

WHY HAS THE CITY'S WATER DRAINED AWAY?

WHO IS THE SEASIDE PRANKSTER?

AND WHY ARE STRANGE POLKA DOTS APPEARING EVERYWHERE?

BOOK FIVE

The pigeons will need to peck punches to solve these mysteries:

WHO STOLE A RARE JEWEL FROM THE WORLD'S FURRIEST MUSEUM?

WILL A HUNGRY WEASEL TRACK DOWN A HIDDEN ENDANGERED BIRD BEFORE THE REAL PIGEONS CAN?

AND HOW DID AN ANCIENT TREE VANISH OVERNIGHT?

BOOK SIX

Can the gang still save the day when they're the ones in trouble?

WHY HAS THE MAYOR BANNED ALL BIRDS?

HOW DOES BREAD BECOME A MONSTER?

CAN BUNNIES BE BOTH EVIL AND CUTE?

REAL PiGEONS

HOW TO DRAW ROCK

1

2

3

4

5

6

7

8

9

10

11

12

FOR DEANNE — ANDREW   FOR KYLIE — BEN

REAL PIGEONS
EAT DANGER

first published in 2018
Hardie Grant Children's Publishing

This edition published in 2021 by Farshore

An imprint of HarperCollins*Publishers*
1 London Bridge Street
London SE1 9GF

HarperCollins*Publishers*
1st Floor, Watermarque Building,
Ringsend Road Dublin 4, Ireland

farshore.co.uk

Text copyright © 2018 Andrew McDonald
Illustration copyright © 2018 Ben Wood
Series design copyright © 2018 Hardie Grant Children's Publishing
Design by Kristy Lund-White

ISBN 9780755501359

Printed and bound in Great Britain by the CPI Group

1

A CIP catalogue record for this title is available from the British Library

MIX
Paper from
responsible sources
FSC™ C007454

FSC
www.fsc.org

This book is produced from independently certified FSC™ paper
to ensure responsible forest management.

For more information visit: www.harpercollins.co.uk/green